Luminescence of Love II

Hoshi - Takashi

M V Tryst

pencil

ISBN 978-93-5667-834-7
© M V Tryst 2023

Published in India 2023 by Pencil

A brand of

One Point Six Technologies Pvt. Ltd.
Unit no. 26, Ground Floor, Building A1,
Wadala Truck Terminal Road,
Near Post Office, Antop Hill, Mumbai - 400037
E connect@thepencilapp.com
W www.thepencilapp.com

Author biography

M V Tryst is the author of 'Luminescence of Love II' Tryst had a good experience in writing and is an eloquent speaker and writer.

Tryst is a student in Finance and Economics.

Tryst is a polyglot and is interested in learning history and cultures across the world.

Tryst loves to learn and share knowledge, and facts about the world through various sources in fictional, non-fictional, and poetic ways.

Tryst's writing style is marked by its authenticity, depth, and unwavering commitment to engaging storytelling. Through thought-provoking narratives, captivating imagery, and profound reflections, the author connects with readers, inviting them to embark on transformative journeys of their own. Tryst's books offer a window into the human experience, inspiring readers to embrace life's adventures, explore the depths of their souls, and evolve into the best versions of themselves.

CONTENTS

Chapter 1 - Fractured Bonds.. 9

Chapter 2 - Rediscovering Love 12

Chapter 3 - The Hidden Letter 15

Chapter 4 - A Glimpse of the Past.. 21

Chapter 5 - Pursuit of Reconciliation 30

Chapter 6 - The Kids' Wish.. 36

Chapter 7 - The Day of Reckoning.. 40

Chapter 8 - A Heart's Last Embrace...................................... 43

Introduction

As the stage transitions from Akira to Isamu, the atmosphere is infused with a sense of reverence and anticipation. All eyes turn towards Isamu, the husband of Akira, as he steps forward to continue the narrative of their family's journey. The room falls silent, eager to hear his perspective and insights, as Isamu takes his place at the podium, ready to share his own profound reflections on the legacy of Hiroshi, Sakura, and the unbreakable bonds that have shaped their lives.

"Ladies, gentlemen, and honoured guests,
Today, as we gather to celebrate the enduring power of love and resilience, I stand before you as Isamu, the husband of Akira and a witness to the remarkable story of my father, Hiroshi, and my aunt, Sakura. Their journey is one that has touched my heart deeply and continues to inspire me every day.

It is with profound gratitude and reverence that I speak of my grandparents, Takashi and Hoshi, who, despite enduring unimaginable pain and loss, found the strength to rebuild their lives and create a legacy of love. Their love story, cut short by the tragedy of war, continues to shine brightly in our hearts.

Takashi, a man of unwavering determination and grace, taught us the importance of never giving up on our dreams. He showed us that love knows no boundaries and that it has the power to heal even the deepest wounds. His love for Hoshi was a beacon of hope, a reminder that no matter how dark the world may seem, love has the power to illuminate our path.

Hoshi, a woman of immense resilience and compassion, taught us the true meaning of strength. In the face of unimaginable loss, she held our family together, becoming a guiding light for my father and my aunt. Her love and guidance continue to shape our lives, reminding us of the importance of cherishing every moment and nurturing the bonds that connect us.

My father, Hiroshi, and my aunt, Sakura, inherited their parents' resilience and love. They carried their legacy forward, forging their own paths and touching the lives of many. They taught us that the scars we bear do not define us, but rather, they serve as reminders of the strength we possess within.

Hiroshi, a visionary architect, created structures that not only stood as testaments to his talent but also embodied the essence of rebuilding and renewal. His designs reflected his belief that even in the face of destruction, beauty can rise from the ashes. He taught us that our actions have the power to shape the world around us and that through creativity and determination, we can leave a lasting impact.

Sakura, a compassionate healer, dedicated her life to serving others. Her love and care touched the lives of countless patients, offering them comfort and hope in their darkest moments. She showed us that true strength lies in our ability to extend compassion and empathy to those in need, and that healing comes not only from medicine but from the power of human connection.

Today, as I stand here, I am reminded of the lessons passed down through generations—the importance of love, resilience, and unity. It is our duty, as the torchbearers of their legacy, to carry these values forward and spread them to the world.

Let us remember the lives of Takashi and Hoshi, Hiroshi and Sakura, and all those who have come before us. May their love and resilience inspire us to live with purpose, to embrace one another with kindness, and to never lose sight of the power of love, even in the darkest of times.

And here's their story...

Chapter 1 - Fractured Bonds

Takashi sat alone in the dimly lit living room, his heart heavy with the weight of unspoken words. As a successful businessman, he had spent countless hours building his empire, striving for financial success and social recognition. But in the pursuit of his ambitions, he had inadvertently neglected the needs of his wife, Hoshi, a diligent and hardworking farmer.

The cracks in their relationship had slowly widened over time, fueled by their diverging paths and the growing distance between them. Takashi's long hours at the office and business travels kept him away from home, leaving Hoshi to tend to their land and family responsibilities on her own. Their once harmonious partnership had been replaced by frustration and resentment.

Takashi often found himself lost in thoughts of Hoshi's radiant smile, the way her hands gently cradled the soil, and the unwavering dedication she poured into her work. He admired her strength and admired the way she nurtured their land with love and care. Despite his success in the corporate world, he felt a pang of longing for the simplicity and groundedness that Hoshi embodied.

Hoshi, on the other hand, carried the weight of her unexpressed desires and dreams. While she had always supported Takashi's pursuit of success, she couldn't help but yearn for a deeper connection—a connection that transcended their respective roles and brought them closer together as partners in life. She longed for Takashi's presence, for his understanding of the beauty and hardships of the land she worked so tirelessly to cultivate.

The distance between them had become a wall that stifled their ability to communicate and understand each other's perspectives. The demands of Takashi's business ventures left little time for meaningful conversations, and Hoshi's exhaustion from farm work left her emotionally drained. They had inadvertently slipped into a pattern of isolation and miscommunication.

Yet, deep within their hearts, there remained an unspoken love—a love that had weathered the storms of life and still yearned to be rekindled. In stolen glances across the dinner table or fleeting moments of tenderness, they caught glimpses of the hidden emotions that lay dormant within them. They sensed that a spark of connection still flickered beneath the layers of hurt and neglect.

As fate would have it, a series of events began to unfold, gradually nudging them toward a path of self-reflection and rediscovery. Chance encounters with wise elders, shared moments of vulnerability with friends, and even the natural beauty of the changing seasons all conspired to awaken something within them.

Takashi started to question the true meaning of success and realized that he had lost sight of the values that truly mattered in life. He began to see Hoshi's immense strength and resilience and the love she poured into their home and land. His heart swelled with a newfound admiration for her unwavering commitment.

Likewise, Hoshi found solace in the simplicity of nature and the connection she felt to the earth. She began to recognize that her own dreams and aspirations had taken a backseat to the demands of their relationship. She yearned for Takashi's support and understanding, a deep-rooted connection that transcended their individual roles.

As the realization dawned upon them, the unexpressed love within their hearts started to bloom, albeit tentatively. They both felt a growing desire to bridge the gap that had formed between them, to reconnect on a deeper level and rebuild what had been lost.

In the depths of their souls, Takashi and Hoshi understood that their journey toward reconciliation would not be easy. It would require them to confront their own shortcomings, communicate their desires and needs, and rebuild the trust that had been eroded over time.

Chapter 2 - Rediscovering Love

With hearts brimming with hope and a newfound determination, Takashi and Hoshi embarked on a journey of rediscovery, one fueled by their shared desire to bridge the gap that had formed between them. The walls of isolation began to crumble as they turned to the power of written words to express their deepest longings.

In the quiet solitude of their respective spaces, Takashi and Hoshi exchanged heartfelt letters. Each stroke of the pen carried the weight of their emotions, their dreams, and their yearning for a future together. They poured their souls onto the paper, baring their vulnerabilities and offering glimpses into the depths of their love.

Takashi's words flowed with a tenderness he had long kept hidden. He confessed his regret for neglecting the person who had been his anchor, and he expressed his fervent desire to make amends. In his letters, he painted vivid pictures of the life they could build together—a life that encompassed the harmony of their shared dreams, their children, and the fertile land that held so much meaning for both of them.

Hoshi's responses were filled with a mix of trepidation and hope. She spoke of the pain they had endured, the tears shed in solitude, and the longing that had never ceased. But amidst the pain, she also found solace in Takashi's words of remorse and his renewed commitment to their relationship. Her letters revealed the flicker of faith she held onto—the belief that love when tended to with care and sincerity, could overcome even the greatest obstacles.

Through their heartfelt correspondence, Takashi and Hoshi began to reimagine their future. They dreamt of a life where their two worlds, once drifting apart, would come together in perfect harmony. They wrote of evenings spent around the dinner table, sharing stories and laughter, and of lazy Sunday mornings where they would walk hand in hand through the fields they both cherished.

They envisioned a life that honored the values they held dear—a life that celebrated the simplicity of their connection and the beauty of their shared endeavors. Their letters were filled with plans to create a home where their children could thrive, their passions could intertwine, and their love would forever be the foundation.

Their hearts slowly mended as the pages filled with their words, and their love grew stronger. Each letter brought them closer, bridging the gap that had once seemed insurmountable. They discovered that their shared dreams and aspirations were not lost but merely waiting to be reignited.

Finally, after a series of heartfelt exchanges, Takashi and Hoshi reached a pivotal moment. They found the courage to discuss meeting again, face to face, to breathe life into the words they had written, and to forge a path toward rebuilding their lives together as a family of four.

With hopeful anticipation, they set a date for their reunion—a place where they would once again be united, not as two separate entities, but as a couple determined to heal the wounds of the past and create a future filled with love, understanding, and unwavering support.

The road ahead was not without its challenges, but armed with the power of their rediscovered love, Takashi and Hoshi embraced the journey that awaited them. They knew that rebuilding their relationship would require time, patience, and a commitment to open and honest communication. But they also knew that the love they had found within their hearts was worth fighting for and that together, they could create a life that surpassed their wildest dreams.

And so, with their pens poised and hearts intertwined, they prepared to take the next step—their reunion, a turning point on their path of rediscovering love and forging a future that held the promise of a love that would endure for a lifetime.

Chapter 3 - The Hidden Letter

Time passed, and the anticipation of their reunion grew stronger with each passing day. Takashi and Hoshi had eagerly awaited this moment, a chance to finally come face to face and reaffirm their love. However, as fate would have it, a sudden and unexpected turn of events threw their plans into disarray.

On a rainy afternoon, as Takashi sat in his office gazing out at the gray skies, a sense of unease washed over him. He couldn't shake off the feeling that something was amiss. An envelope, slightly damp and tattered, caught his attention on the corner of his desk. Curiosity piqued, he carefully opened it, revealing a letter written in elegant handwriting.

The words on the page sent shivers down Takashi's spine. It was a letter from Hoshi—an unspoken letter, hidden away until now. She poured out her heart into it, expressing her deepest fears and doubts about their reunion. She confessed her struggle to fully trust in their love, still haunted by the pain of their past disconnect.

Hoshi's letter revealed a vulnerability that Takashi had only glimpsed in fleeting moments. She wrote of the sleepless nights, the tears shed in solitude, and the lingering doubts that had plagued her. It was a confession of the scars she carried and her fear of being hurt once more.

As Takashi read her words, his heart ached with a mix of remorse and understanding. He realized that their journey toward rediscovering love was not just about rebuilding what they had lost but also about healing the wounds they inflicted upon each other. Hoshi's letter served as a poignant reminder of the importance of patience, empathy, and the need to address their past before embracing their future.

With a newfound sense of purpose, Takashi picked up his pen and wrote his response—a letter filled with reassurance, empathy, and unwavering commitment. He poured his heart onto the page, acknowledging Hoshi's pain and promising to do everything in his power to mend the broken pieces of their relationship.

In his letter, Takashi spoke of his own insecurities and regrets, opening up about the sacrifices he had made and the toll it had taken on their connection. He assured Hoshi that he was fully committed to their reunion, ready to face the challenges head-on, and dedicated to creating a safe space where their love could flourish once more.

Days turned into weeks as their correspondence continued. Through their letters, they delved into the depths of their emotions, unraveling the layers of hurt and insecurity that had long been buried. They shared their dreams and aspirations, their visions of a future where their love would stand unbreakable, a beacon of hope for their children and generations to come.

With each letter exchanged, Takashi and Hoshi discovered a renewed sense of understanding, a deeper connection that had eluded them in the past. Their words became a testament to their growth, a testament to the strength of their love and their unwavering commitment to one another.

Finally, the day of their long-awaited reunion arrived. Takashi and Hoshi stood face to face, their eyes mirroring a mix of nervousness and anticipation. Their letters paved the way for this moment, but it was their shared journey of self-reflection, forgiveness, and open communication that had brought them here.

In that moment, as they embraced, they felt a profound sense of gratitude—gratitude for the hidden letter that had revealed their innermost fears and paved the way for healing. It was a reminder that love, when nurtured with honesty and vulnerability, had the power to overcome even the greatest of obstacles.

With their hearts intertwined and their souls reconnected, Takashi and Hoshi embarked on a new chapter of their life together. The wounds of the past were not forgotten, but they served as a reminder of the importance of nurturing their love and prioritizing their connection above all else.

Takashi and Hoshi made a pact to create a new beginning, to build a life that honored their individual dreams and aspirations while fostering a deep sense of togetherness. They recognized that their reunion was not the end of their journey but rather the start of a continuous effort to nurture their relationship.

In the days that followed, they set out to create a home filled with love, compassion, and understanding. They carved out moments of shared laughter, exploring the simple joys of life that had been overshadowed by their previous pursuits. They took long walks hand in hand, allowing the beauty of nature to rekindle their spirits and ignite a sense of wonder in their hearts.

Together, Takashi and Hoshi made a conscious effort to communicate openly and honestly, creating a safe space where their thoughts, desires, and fears could be freely expressed. They celebrated each other's victories, supporting and encouraging one another in their individual endeavors.

As time passed, their love story began to weave itself into the very fabric of their lives. Takashi actively participated in the farming duties, his tailored suits replaced by sturdy overalls. He marveled at the hard work and dedication that Hoshi had poured into their land, and he became an unwavering source of support in her pursuit of innovation and sustainable farming practices.

In turn, Hoshi discovered a renewed sense of purpose within their partnership. She found inspiration in Takashi's business acumen and sought to create a harmonious balance between the land and the world of commerce. Together, they envisioned a future where their combined strengths would create a legacy that extended beyond their own lives.

Their children, who had silently observed the transformation of their parents' love, reveled in the newfound warmth and harmony that now permeated their home. Takashi and Hoshi shared with their children the journey they had undertaken to rediscover their love, teaching them the value of resilience, forgiveness, and the importance of nurturing relationships.

In the quiet moments of their evenings, Takashi and Hoshi would often sit on the porch, looking out at the land they had cultivated together. With their hands entwined, they marveled at the beauty of their shared journey—the highs and lows, the tears and laughter, and the unyielding love that had weathered it all.

Their love story had emerged from the shadows, blossoming into a testament of hope and renewal. Takashi and Hoshi had discovered that the most profound love was not found in grand gestures or extravagant displays but rather in the small, everyday acts of kindness, understanding, and unwavering commitment to one another.

As their love continued to evolve, Takashi and Hoshi vowed to remain vigilant—to always nurture their connection, to never take each other for granted, and to never let the busyness of life overshadow the flame of their love. They had learned that love was not a destination but a continuous journey—an ever-unfolding story that required constant attention, care, and the willingness to grow together.

And so, they embarked on this journey with open hearts, knowing that their love had triumphed over the obstacles that had once threatened to tear them apart. With each passing day, their love grew stronger, and their commitment to each other deepened.

Together, they wrote a new chapter filled with rediscovered love, shared dreams, and the infinite possibilities that awaited them.

Chapter 4 - A Glimpse of the Past

The warm afternoon sun cast a golden glow over Takashi and Hoshi's peaceful countryside home. It had been several years since they had embarked on their journey of rediscovering love, and their bond had grown deeper with each passing day. Yet, as content as they were in the present, there was still a lingering curiosity about their shared history, the untold stories that shaped their lives.

One day, while sorting through a dusty box in the attic, Takashi stumbled upon a stack of old letters tied together with a faded ribbon. Intrigued, he carefully untied the ribbon and began to read the handwritten words penned by Hoshi's late grandmother.

As he delved into the heartfelt letters, a profound sense of connection washed over Takashi. Through the words on those weathered pages, he caught a glimpse of Hoshi's lineage, her family's struggles, and their unwavering spirit. Each letter was filled with love, resilience, and a deep sense of gratitude for the simple joys of life.

Eager to share this newfound treasure with Hoshi, Takashi rushed downstairs, letter in hand. With anticipation in his voice, he called out for her, and Hoshi appeared, curiosity etched across her face. Seeing the letters clutched in

Takashi's hands, her eyes widened with a mix of surprise and excitement.

As they sat side by side, enveloped in the warmth of their shared love, Takashi began to read aloud the poignant words that Hoshi's grandmother had written so many years ago. The stories painted a vivid picture of the struggles and triumphs that had shaped their family's journey through life.

With each passing letter, Takashi and Hoshi felt their hearts open wider, embracing not only their own histories but also the legacies of those who had come before them. The stories became a bridge, connecting the present with the past, and igniting a renewed appreciation for their roots.

Through those letters, they discovered the shared values that had been passed down through generations. The unwavering dedication to family, the resilience in the face of adversity, and the unyielding belief in the power of love and unity. It was as if the spirits of their ancestors were whispering wisdom and guidance, reminding them of the strength they possessed.

Embracing the significance of their shared heritage, Takashi and Hoshi made a vow to honor their ancestors' legacy and build a future that embodied their values. They realized that their love was not just their own but a culmination of the love that had thrived in their families for generations.

As they continued reading the letters, tears welled up in their eyes, their hearts overflowing with gratitude for the lives they had been given. They saw their own reflections in the struggles and joys described in the letters, and they knew that their connection ran deeper than they could have ever imagined.

In that moment, Takashi and Hoshi understood the power of their love—the unbreakable thread that connected them to their past and propelled them forward into the future. They vowed to live each day with intention, cherishing the moments they had together and nurturing their love as a testament to the love that had come before them.

With the letters serving as a constant reminder of their shared heritage, Takashi and Hoshi felt a renewed sense of purpose. They understood that their love story was not just about them but about honoring their ancestors and paving the way for future generations.

As they closed the last letter, a profound sense of peace settled over them. They knew that their journey of rediscovering love was far from over, but armed with the wisdom and strength gleaned from the past, they were ready to face any challenge that lay ahead.

Surrounded by the echoes of their family's stories, Takashi and Hoshi made a promise to themselves and to each other. They would preserve their shared heritage and pass it down to their children, ensuring that the lessons of love, resilience, and gratitude would endure.

Inspired by the letters, they decided to create a family tradition of storytelling, where they would gather around the fireplace and share tales of their ancestors. They would weave together the narratives of triumphs and hardships, of love and sacrifice, painting a rich tapestry of their family's history.

As the years went by, Takashi and Hoshi faithfully upheld this tradition, nurturing a deep sense of belonging and connection within their family. Their children grew up with a profound appreciation for their roots, understanding the sacrifices made by their ancestors and the importance of cherishing their heritage.

With their newfound appreciation for their past, Takashi and Hoshi also realized the significance of living fully in the present. They made a conscious effort to prioritize quality time together, carving out moments in their busy lives to truly connect and strengthen their bond.

They took long walks hand in hand through the fields, marveling at the beauty of nature and finding solace in each other's presence. They sat beneath the stars on warm summer nights, sharing dreams and aspirations, rekindling the spark of passion that had brought them together.

Through their shared experiences and open communication, Takashi and Hoshi continued to deepen their understanding of one another. They embraced their differences and celebrated their unique strengths, recognizing that their individual journeys had only enriched their love.

Their renewed commitment to each other extended beyond their own relationship. They sought opportunities to give back to their community, support local farmers and promote sustainable practices. Together, they found fulfillment in nurturing not only their own love but also the world around them.

As they embraced the values passed down through generations, Takashi and Hoshi found that their love grew stronger with each passing day. They realized that true success wasn't measured solely by financial achievements or societal recognition but by the depth of their connection and the positive impact they could make in the lives of others.

Their journey of rediscovering love had brought them full circle—back to the core of what truly mattered. It was no longer just about their individual ambitions, but about creating a legacy of love, compassion, and shared experiences for their children and future generations.

Takashi and Hoshi's story became a testament to the power of resilience, forgiveness, and the unbreakable bonds of love. They had journeyed through the depths of their hearts, confronting their own shortcomings, and emerged stronger and more united than ever before.

As they looked toward the future, their hearts brimming with hope, Takashi and Hoshi knew that their love story would continue to evolve. They had learned that love was not a static destination but a lifelong journey of growth, understanding, and endless possibilities.

Together, they embraced the unknown with open arms, ready to face whatever challenges and adventures lay ahead. Hand in hand, they walked forward, guided by the wisdom of their past, the strength of their love, and the promise of a future filled with endless love, joy, and shared dreams.

The differences that initially arose between Takashi and Hoshi were rooted in their respective paths and responsibilities in life. Takashi, as a successful businessman, was consumed by the demands of his career. He dedicated long hours to building his empire, pursuing financial success, and seeking social recognition. His ambition and drive led him to prioritize work above all else, including his relationship with Hoshi.

On the other hand, Hoshi, as a hardworking farmer, devoted herself to the land and their family responsibilities. She poured her energy and love into nurturing the crops, tending to their home, and ensuring the well-being of their children. The physical demands of farm work left her exhausted, both physically and emotionally, and there was little time for her own personal pursuits or desires.

The diverging paths and the demands of their respective roles created a growing distance between Takashi and Hoshi. Their daily routines became disconnected, with Takashi focused on his business ventures and Hoshi shouldering the burden of the farm work. They had less time for meaningful conversations, shared experiences, and understanding each other's perspectives.

The lack of communication and understanding led to frustration and resentment. Takashi's absence from home, coupled with Hoshi's exhaustion, made it difficult for them to connect on a deeper level. The emotional and physical distance between them gradually eroded their bond, and they found themselves slipping into a pattern of isolation and miscommunication.

Additionally, their different lifestyles and priorities led to a divergence in their values and aspirations. Takashi was driven by material success, seeking validation through his professional achievements, while Hoshi found fulfillment and purpose in the simplicity and connection to the land. Their contrasting perspectives on what constituted success and happiness further contributed to the growing divide between them.

Ultimately, it was the accumulation of these differences, coupled with their neglect of each other's needs, that created a rift in their relationship. They became disconnected from one another, their dreams, and the core values that had once united them. However, it was through their journey of rediscovery and self-reflection that they began to bridge these differences and rebuild their love.

As the distance between Takashi and Hoshi grew, their children, Hiroshi and Sakura, found themselves caught in the crossfire of their parents' strained relationship. While both parents loved their children deeply, their preoccupation with their own issues and lack of emotional connection affected their ability to provide the love and attention their children needed.

Hiroshi, at the age of five, and Sakura, at six, were too young to fully understand the complexities of their parents' situation. They yearned for their parents' love, care, and presence in their lives, but their parents' emotional distance made it difficult for them to feel secure and valued. The children often witnessed their parents' arguments and felt the tension that permeated the household, creating a sense of unease and confusion.

Takashi, consumed by his business pursuits, spent minimal time at home. His long working hours and frequent travels meant that he missed out on important milestones and everyday moments in his children's lives. He struggled to connect with Hiroshi and Sakura on a deeper level, unaware of their emotional needs and desires. In their young minds, Takashi's absence translated into a lack of love and attention.

Similarly, Hoshi, burdened by the responsibilities of the farm and household, found herself overwhelmed and exhausted. While she showered Hiroshi and Sakura with care and met their basic needs, the emotional strain she experienced in her relationship with Takashi made it challenging for her to fully engage with her children. Her own unmet desires and frustrations occasionally spilled over into her interactions with them, unintentionally causing emotional distress.

As a result, Hiroshi and Sakura yearned for their parents' affection, longing for their attention and approval. They witnessed other families where parents were actively involved in their children's lives, creating a sense of envy and deep sadness within them. The lack of parental love and connection affected their self-esteem and emotional well-being, leaving them feeling a sense of emptiness and abandonment.

Despite their young age, Hiroshi and Sakura were perceptive enough to recognize the tension between their parents. They internalized their parents' struggles and blamed themselves for the growing distance between Takashi and Hoshi. The absence of a loving and nurturing family environment left them feeling adrift and uncertain, impacting their sense of security and trust in the world.

It was within this context of parental neglect and emotional void that Hiroshi and Sakura's childhood unfolded. Their innocence and vulnerability made them silent witnesses to their parents' struggles, their unspoken desires for their parents' love leaving a lasting impact on their lives.

Chapter 5 - Pursuit of Reconciliation

Takashi and Hoshi found themselves at a crossroads, their hearts heavy with the realization of the impact their fractured relationship had on their children and their own well-being. Fueled by a newfound determination, they embarked on a journey of reconciliation, hoping to mend the broken bonds that had kept them apart for far too long.

They began by acknowledging their individual contributions to the distance that had formed between them. With open hearts and a willingness to confront their own shortcomings, they engaged in honest conversations, expressing their deepest fears, frustrations, and desires. It was a vulnerable process, but one that was essential for them to heal and move forward.

Takashi recognized the importance of prioritizing his family over his career aspirations. He made a conscious effort to restructure his work-life balance, carving out dedicated time for his children and Hoshi. He actively participated in their lives, attending school events, helping with homework, and engaging in heartfelt conversations. Through these actions, he aimed to rebuild the trust and connection that had been eroded over time.

Hoshi, too, committed herself to nurturing the emotional bond with Takashi. She shared her dreams and aspirations, allowing Takashi to see the depth of her desires beyond their roles as parents and providers. She revealed her vulnerability, expressing her need for his understanding, support, and presence in their children's lives. Hoshi's honesty and vulnerability touched Takashi's heart, making him realize the depth of her love and the importance of their partnership.

Together, Takashi and Hoshi explored various avenues to reignite their shared interests and find common ground. They embarked on adventures as a family, discovering new hobbies and activities that allowed them to connect on a deeper level. Whether it was tending to the garden together, exploring the beauty of nature, or cooking meals as a family, they found solace in the simple joys of shared experiences.

In their pursuit of reconciliation, they sought guidance from wise elders and professionals who helped them navigate the intricacies of rebuilding their relationship. They attended counseling sessions, where they learned effective communication techniques, strategies for resolving conflicts, and ways to foster empathy and understanding. These sessions became instrumental in their journey toward healing, offering them tools to navigate the challenges that lay ahead.

The journey of reconciliation was not without its setbacks and moments of doubt. There were times when old wounds resurfaced, threatening to pull them back into familiar patterns of miscommunication and isolation. Yet, their love for each other and their commitment to their children's well-being propelled them forward. They refused to let their past define their future, determined to create a loving and nurturing environment for their family.

Slowly but surely, Takashi and Hoshi began to witness the positive impact their efforts had on their children. Hiroshi and Sakura, once withdrawn and longing for their parents' love, started to bloom in the presence of their reconciling parents. They felt the warmth of their parents' affection, the stability of their united front, and the assurance that they were loved unconditionally.

Through their pursuit of reconciliation, Takashi and Hoshi discovered that forgiveness and understanding were key ingredients in rebuilding their relationship. They learned to let go of past grievances, choosing compassion and empathy instead. They recognized that their individual growth and healing were essential for their partnership to thrive, and they supported each other in their personal journeys.

Takashi and Hoshi found themselves on the cusp of a new beginning. The pursuit of reconciliation had brought them closer than ever before, and the love that had once been hidden beneath layers of hurt and neglect now radiated through their actions and words. With their hearts aligned and their commitment renewed, they stood ready to embrace the future, united as a family that had emerged from the depths of adversity.

In the midst of their pursuit of reconciliation, Takashi and Hoshi realized the importance of creating new traditions and rituals that would strengthen their bond as a family. They established a weekly family night where they would gather together, free from distractions, to engage in activities that fostered laughter, joy, and genuine connection. These moments became cherished memories that helped solidify their newfound closeness.

They also made a conscious effort to prioritize quality time with each child individually. Takashi took Hiroshi on hiking trips, encouraging his adventurous spirit and providing a safe space for him to share his thoughts and dreams. Hoshi, on the other hand, spent quiet evenings with Sakura, nurturing her creativity through art projects and listening attentively to her stories. These one-on-one moments allowed them to truly understand and appreciate the unique qualities of each child.

As their love and connection continued to deepen, Takashi and Hoshi made a conscious decision to be more mindful and present in their daily interactions. They put aside their phones and committed to actively listening to one another, offering support and validation. Through these small but meaningful gestures, they slowly rebuilt the trust and intimacy that had been eroded over the years.

The journey of reconciliation extended beyond the confines of their immediate family. Takashi and Hoshi actively sought opportunities to give back to their community, recognizing the power of compassion and service in healing not only their own wounds but also those of others. They engaged in volunteer work together, lending their time and resources to local organizations that supported families in need. By extending their love and support beyond their own household, they discovered a deeper sense of purpose and fulfillment.

Throughout their pursuit of reconciliation, Takashi and Hoshi remained committed to open and honest communication. They established a habit of regular check-ins, where they would sit down to discuss their emotions, concerns, and aspirations. These conversations allowed them to address any lingering doubts or fears, providing a safe space for vulnerability and understanding. They learned to approach conflicts with empathy and actively sought resolution through compromise and collaboration.

As time passed, their efforts bore fruit. The wounds of the past gradually healed, replaced by a renewed sense of love, trust, and respect. Takashi and Hoshi marveled at the transformation they had undergone as individuals and as a couple. They realized that their journey toward reconciliation was not a destination but a continuous process of growth and renewal.

With their children as witnesses to their shared transformation, Takashi and Hoshi became role models of resilience, forgiveness, and the power of love. Their story served as a reminder that no matter how broken a relationship may seem, with dedication, patience, and a genuine desire to understand one another, it is possible to rebuild what was once lost.

Takashi and Hoshi stood side by side, their hearts brimming with gratitude for the second chance they had been given. They embraced the future with hope, knowing that their journey of reconciliation had not only brought them back together but had also created a foundation of love and understanding that would carry them forward, hand in hand, for the rest of their lives.

Chapter 6 - The Kids' Wish

As Takashi and Hoshi work on themselves, their home starts to transform. Laughter and joy make a comeback, replacing the gloom that once lingered. Their renewed love inspires others, giving hope to those going through similar struggles.

But they understand that reconciliation is an ongoing process. It requires constant effort and a willingness to address their shortcomings. They face each challenge together, knowing that their love can overcome any darkness.

With each step forward, Takashi and Hoshi grow stronger. They emerge from the shadows with a deepened bond and a renewed commitment to each other. Their journey reminds them of their resilience and the power of love to overcome obstacles.

They embrace the future with hope and determination, ready to face whatever comes their way. The shadows that once haunted them now serve as reminders of their strength and the depths of their love.

As the sun sets on this chapter, a new one begins. Takashi and Hoshi move forward, hand in hand, leaving behind the darkness and embracing the light that awaits them.

The day after the shadows began to dissipate, a ray of sunlight entered Hiroshi and Sakura's hearts. Excitement bubbled within them as they hatched a plan that would change their parents' lives forever.

In the morning, as Takashi and Hoshi sat down for breakfast, Hiroshi and Sakura couldn't contain their anticipation any longer. With hopeful eyes and nervous smiles, they mustered the courage to voice their heartfelt request.

"Dad, Mom," Hiroshi began, his voice filled with determination. "We've been watching you two rediscover your love. It's been beautiful to witness. And... we want you to get married again."

Sakura nodded eagerly, her voice joining her brother's. "Yes, we want to see our family whole again. We want to see you both happy and together, just like before."
Takashi and Hoshi exchanged surprised glances, their hearts swelling with both joy and apprehension. They never expected their children to make such a heartfelt plea. It was a testament to the love they had been slowly rebuilding.

Tears welled up in Hoshi's eyes as she reached out to embrace her children. "Oh, my darlings," she whispered, her voice choked with emotion. "Your love and support mean the world to us. We will consider your wish very seriously."

Takashi, too, was moved by their children's unwavering faith. "You two are the light of our lives," he said, his voice trembling. "We will honor your request and take it to heart. Let's see what the future holds for us."

As the day unfolded, Takashi and Hoshi couldn't help but reflect on their children's words. The thought of remarriage brought a mix of excitement and trepidation. They knew it was a significant step, one that required careful consideration and a genuine desire to rebuild their lives together.

In the quiet of the evening, as the family gathered around the dinner table, Takashi and Hoshi shared their decision with Hiroshi and Sakura. With smiles on their faces and renewed hope in their hearts, they announced, "Tomorrow, we will begin a new chapter in our lives. We will renew our vows and recommit to our love for each other." They wanted this event to be among the four of them.

The children erupted in cheers and embraced their parents tightly. The joy and love that filled the room were undeniable, a testament to the power of healing and the resilience of their family.

As they prepared for bed that night, Hiroshi and Sakura whispered their gratitude to the stars above. Their innocent hearts had seen what their parents couldn't at times, the unwavering love that bound them together.

The next day, Takashi and Hoshi stood together once more, ready to declare their commitment to one anotherofficially. With Hiroshi and Sakura by their side, they spoke their vows, promising to cherish and nurture their love forever.

The shadows of the past were completely lifted, replaced by a radiant light that illuminated their path. As a family, they embarked on a new journey, united in love and ready to embrace the future that awaited them.

Chapter 7 - The Day of Reckoning

The day had finally arrived—the day when Takashi and Hoshi would solemnize their love once again in the presence of their loved ones. A beautiful morning in Nagasaki, the serene and picturesque location, a lush garden nestled amidst blooming flowers and towering trees, had been carefully chosen to symbolize the renewal of their bond.

The air was filled with anticipation and joy as family and friends gathered, eagerly awaiting the moment when Hiroshi would walk his mother down the aisle, and Sakura would accompany her father. It was a heartfelt gesture from the children, a symbol of their unwavering support for their parents' reconciliation.

As the time drew near, Hiroshi took his mother's arm, a mix of pride and emotion visible in his eyes. Sakura, her small hand clasped tightly in her father's, radiated pure happiness. Together, they began their walk towards the flower-adorned aisle, where Takashi stood, his heart brimming with love and hope.

The sun bathed the garden in a golden glow, casting a serene ambiance over the scene. Tears of joy glistened in the eyes of the guests, moved by the profound love and resilience displayed by this family. It was a moment of pure beauty, where wounds were healing, and hearts were reconnecting.

But as Hiroshi and Sakura reached the midway point of the aisle, their joy turned to horror. A deafening blast shattered the tranquility, ripping through the air and engulfing everything in chaos. The force of the explosion sent shockwaves through the gathering, knocking people off their feet and filling the once-serene atmosphere with screams and cries of pain.

Amidst the chaos, Hiroshi, Sakura, and Hoshi were left disoriented and injured, their bodies bruised and bleeding. The full extent of the tragedy slowly unfolded before their eyes—the lifeless body of Takashi lay motionless, his eyes closed forever.

Time stood still as grief washed over them, intertwining with the shattered fragments of their dreams. The garden that was once a symbol of renewal had become a haunting reminder of the fragility of life.

In the days that followed, the family clung to each other for solace and support. The physical wounds would heal, but the emotional scars ran deep. They mourned the loss of Takashi, a man who had rediscovered his love and was taken from them in an instant.

The bombing had left an indelible mark on their lives. The questions of why and who remained unanswered, adding to their grief and fueling a growing desire for justice. They vowed to find the truth and bring those responsible to account, not only for their own healing but for the memory of Takashi.

Through their pain, Hiroshi and Sakura found strength in one another. They became each other's pillars, supporting their mother in her darkest moments. Together, they embarked on a journey of healing, navigating the complexities of grief and loss.

In the midst of their grief, a flicker of determination ignited within the family. They knew that Takashi would have wanted them to carry on, to find solace in the love they shared and the memories they cherished. It was their way of honoring his spirit, of keeping his legacy alive.

As they faced the day of reckoning, the family resolved to let love guide them. They vowed to live their lives with purpose, to find meaning in the midst of tragedy. They would continue the pursuit of justice for Takashi while holding onto the love that had brought them together.

In the depths of their pain, they found a renewed sense of unity and resilience. The journey ahead would be arduous, but they were not alone. With the support of their loved ones and the strength they drew from each other, they would navigate the path of healing

Chapter 8 - A Heart's Last Embrace

In the wake of the devastating bombing that had shattered their world, Hiroshi, Sakura, and Hoshi found themselves grappling with the profound grief of losing their beloved father and the wounds that still plagued their bodies. The weight of their pain seemed almost insurmountable, and yet they clung to each other, seeking solace and strength in their shared love.

As days passed, Hoshi's health began to decline. The injuries she sustained in the bombing took a toll on her fragile body. Despite her weakened state, her spirit remained unwavering, and her love for her children burned brightly in her eyes.

Gathered around her bedside, Hiroshi and Sakura held their mother's hands, their hearts heavy with both sorrow and gratitude. They treasured these precious moments, cherishing the time they had left together as a family. It was in these final moments that Hoshi, with her voice barely a whisper, imparted her last words of wisdom.

With love emanating from her every breath, Hoshi spoke of the importance of family, urging Hiroshi and Sakura to remain united through life's trials. She emphasized the strength they derived from their bond, encouraging them to lean on each other for support and to cherish the love that had carried them through their darkest moments.

Hoshi's voice quivered with emotion as she shared memories of their father, recounting his dreams and aspirations for their future. She implored Hiroshi and Sakura to honor their father's legacy by living lives filled with compassion, resilience, and purpose. It was a legacy of love that she entrusted to their care.

In her final moments, Hoshi's eyes sparkled with a mix of sadness and peace. She embraced her children, drawing them close, and whispered her last goodbye. Her last breath became a symbol of her unconditional love, passing the torch of strength and resilience to Hiroshi and Sakura.

As Hoshi slipped away, a profound stillness settled over the room. Hiroshi and Sakura clung to each other, their hearts heavy with grief, but also filled with a renewed sense of purpose. In their mother's final embrace, they had witnessed the indomitable power of love, and they were determined to carry her teachings forward.

In the days that followed, Hiroshi and Sakura mourned their parents' passing, their grief entwined with a newfound resolve to honor their memory. They would face the world together, drawing strength from the unbreakable bond they shared. They would embrace life's challenges with grace, knowing that their parents' love would guide them through.

In the years that followed, Hiroshi and Sakura carried their parents' legacy within their hearts. They became beacons of love and compassion in their community, extending a helping hand to those in need and embodying the lessons their parents had taught them. Their shared experiences and unwavering support for one another created a powerful force that inspired others to find strength in their journeys of healing.

Though the pain of loss remained, Hiroshi and Sakura found solace in the memories and love that their parents had left behind. They continued to hold each other close, cherishing the family they had become and honoring the legacy of their parents with every step they took.

In the embrace of their mother's last breath, Hiroshi and Sakura had discovered a resilience they never knew existed—a strength that would carry them through the darkest of times and guide them toward a future filled with love, purpose, and the unwavering bond of family.

Years had passed since that fateful day when the bombing had forever altered the lives of Hiroshi, Sakura, and Hoshi. The wounds of the past had healed, leaving scars that served as reminders of the strength and resilience they had discovered within themselves.

Hiroshi had become a renowned architect, his designs inspired by the beauty and fragility of life. Each structure he crafted stood as a testament to the power of rebuilding and the importance of cherishing the present moment. Sakura had followed her passion for medicine, dedicating her life to healing others. Her compassion and empathy touched the lives of countless patients, offering them hope and solace.

Together, they had formed a tight-knit family, a refuge in a world that often seemed chaotic and uncertain. They had vowed to honor their parents' memory, and their actions reflected the love and wisdom imparted by their mother and father.

In the garden where their parents' renewal had been shattered, a memorial stood tall—a symbol of the family's resilience and a tribute to the lives lost. It was a place where visitors could find solace and reflect on the enduring power of love in the face of adversity.

Hiroshi and Sakura passed on their parents' teachings to their children, instilling in them the importance of compassion, unity, and the pursuit of justice. The legacy of love had been carried forward, generation after generation, weaving a tapestry of strength and kindness that touched the lives of countless individuals.

In the embrace of their family, Hiroshi and Sakura found solace and joy. They knew that their parents were watching over them, guiding them from the ethereal realm. Their love had transcended time and space, forever intertwined with the lives of their children and grandchildren.

As the sun set over the horizon, casting a warm glow over the garden, Hiroshi and Sakura stood hand in hand, a testament to the enduring power of love. They gazed at the memorial, reflecting on their journey of healing, growth, and resilience.

The legacy of their parents lived on, not just in the structures they built or the lives they touched but in the hearts of all those who had been inspired by their story. And in that final embrace, as the day turned to dusk, Hiroshi and Sakura knew that love would forever be their guiding light, illuminating the path ahead with hope and grace.
And so their story continued, a testament to the unbreakable bonds of family, the indomitable spirit of resilience, and the eternal power of love that transcends even the darkest of days.

My dad and aunt taught the biggest lesson for us by showing their willpower to lead life even losing their whole support system and loved ones. If it was possible for them, then it is, for anyone. Everything happens for a reason. Standing strong is what matters.

Thank you."